LAROONS

CHAOS

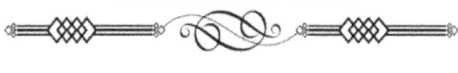

Denise Rader

ASA PUBLISHING CORPORATION

AN INNOVATIVE OUTSOURCE BOOK PUBLISHING HYBRID

ASA Publishing Corporation
1285 N. Telegraph Rd., #351, Monroe, Michigan 48162
An Accredited Publishing House with the BBB
www.asapublishingcorporation.com

Copyrights©2025, Denise Rader, All Rights Reserved
Book Title: Laroons: CHAOS
Date Published: 06.07.2025
Book ID: ASAPCID2380926
Edition: 1 *Trade Paperback*
ISBN: 978-1-960104-77-9
Library of Congress Cataloging-in-Publication Data

This book was published in the United States of America.
Great State of Michigan

Chapter

8

It's 9 AM and Dashan has a lot on his mind because today is this special day that his family has been talking about since last year. He knows it has to be something big because no one will even give him a clue as to what is supposed to happen tonight at 12 PM. Dashan has three major problems that he and only he can solve, and the outcome may not be the one he wants or needs right now in his life. His biggest problem is telling Shauinina about him and Latrain the night of their wedding, then there is the next problem of telling his new and lovely wife the truth about him and his family being vampires, and dealing with these reactions.

Then there is this big day that he has to get ready for. Dashan knows this day or night must be very special because his grandparents, cousins, and uncle will be flying in just for this special occasion. Dashan has a strange feeling that something is wrong but he doesn't know what it is, all he knows is he has a sudden urge to take a walk, as he is walking he notices a road that seems very familiar to him but he can't place it so, he proceeds down this long road and hears what sounds like children riding bikes, but he just shakes it off and starts to turn back around when he suddenly sees three children coming up the road that he is on. Dashan quickly hides behind a large tree as the children, two boys and a girl, ride right pass him. He follows the kids as they speed and whisper to each other on their bikes. Dashan doesn't like to move this slowly because it irritates him, but he knows that he must take it slow to find out what these three are up to. Noah, Ezar, and Cha'nnel decided to see what all the rumors are about an old spooky road that leads to an abandoned shed that is haunted by vampires or ghosts.

The three best friends decide to have some fun and explore the shed for themselves. As they get closer to the shed, they notice that it is farther away than it was when they saw it on the road. The children are very cautious because they don't want to get in trouble, just in case they are on private property and end up getting shot at. Dashan is right on their trail when he suddenly stops and notices four dark figures following the children towards the abandoned shed. Noah, Ezar, and Cha'nnel keep going through the woods and finally come to the shed, but they can sense that something or someone is following them. But, being children, they proceed on and open the shed to find it abandoned.

Two of the figures follow the children while the other two fall back and wait for Dashan to get closer so they can attack him. The children all enter and leave the door wide open just in case they have to make a quick break for it. When the door closes on its own and all three kids are locked inside, they huddle together, and each is about to scream, but they can't because they notice the black figures with red eyes; they are frozen with fear. Dashan approaches the shed, and as he is about to open the door, the three children come running out screaming and ran right into him. Dashan asked them if they were alright, and they told him that there are ghosts with red eyes in there. Dashan tells the kids to get on their bikes and ride as fast as they can, and don't stop until they get home; he will handle the ghosts and meet them at their house to let them know everything is alright.

Noah, Ezar, and Cha'nnel do as they are told and ride on their bikes as fast as they can, and they don't look back until they get home safely, or will they be safe? And who is the guy that saved them? Could he be the owner of the shed and just scare them away? Only time will tell. As Dashan enters the shed the other two black figures approaches and when they get up close enough to look inside the door they notice who it is and they send a message to the other two figures inside the shed to quickly vanish because "the one" is near but, how can that be and if it is true how come the other elders didn't notify them of him coming. Dashan can sense that something is not right about this shed and these woods, but he just doesn't know what it is yet, so he decides to leave quickly just in case this is a set up to kidnap him. Dashan makes his way to the house of Noah where the other two are also, he explains to them that what they saw was all a dream and this day never happened.

It's around 11:00 AM when he returns home and finds his whole family in the living room, the only ones that are not present are the cousins, and he knows why because they don't need to meet the family just yet. They all greeted each other with lots of hugs and kisses, then Mom and Dad asked Dashan where he had been. he just answered that he had taken a walk to clear his mind because he had some big decisions to make today, and he needed to be very clear and levelheaded when making those decisions.

Dashan grandparents Mommy and PopPop is so glad to see all of their grandsons as everyone is starting to get caught up, PopPop ask Dashan "Son have you told your wife your secret?" everyone suddenly gets real quiet and looks directly at Dashan, he answers "no not yet I am scared of what she will say and do ." Mommy tells him that he has to tell her before 12 PM, and he agrees. Dashan asks his grandparents if they know what is so special about today and what happens at 12 PM tonight. They just looked at each other and said, "You will know soon, grandson." Dashan just shrugged it off and went into his room to relax for a minute, but ended up falling asleep.

When he wakes, it's almost 2 PM. Dashan tells his brothers that he is going to need some protection and that it will be good if Boné have his team at the hospital on call waiting and ready for the events that's about to unfold, Boné agrees to let them know and everyone starts to prepare for the heartache and pain that is about to ensure. Rah wants to have the other ladies present for the first part and then have only Shauinina present for the last part if she isn't in jail by then for double murder.

TeeJay, Boné, and Rah all ask Dashan if he is ready for what's about to happen, and he tells them, "No, but it has to be done." Around 3 PM, Dashan lets the family know that there will be a change of plans. Instead of telling Shauinina right away, he is going to make love to her first, since he was too drunk on their wedding night and decided to sleep with the enemy.

His cousin Nigh suggested that because Shauinina will only feel worse and more resentful. Dashan disagrees with Nigh and proceeds with his plan, because he knows his wife will be mad, but she'll never break his heart by leaving him; he can deal with the cussing and fighting (maybe).

Shauinina comes over to the house to see what this big surprise that Dashan has for her. When she arrives, Dashan directs her to their bedroom and apologizes again for getting so drunk on their wedding night. Shauinina forgives him again but tells him he can make it up to her now, and Dashan gladly accepts her offer, as they are making love, Shauinina is crying because it's her first time, plus she's trying to get Dashan to stop because of the intense pain. Dashan finally realizes what is going on with her, and he stops and asks her if he is being too rough. Shauinina says, "No, baby, it's just so painful, is it supposed to hurt this much?" Dashan tells her to try to relax a little more, and it won't hurt as much. She does, and it doesn't help at all. Shauinina tells Dashan, "Baby, just go as fast as you can so you can pop my cherry and the pain can stop."

Dashan does as she asks. He then notices a strong smell of blood, and he knows it's from Shauinina. He starts to feel a hunger for her, not for her body, but for her blood. Dashan quickly jumps off her and runs in the bathroom to splash cold water on his face. When he looks in the mirror, he notices that his eyes have changed to a reddish-orange color, and his headaches are returning. He hears Shauinina coming towards the bathroom, so he quickly jumps into the shower so he doesn't face her. Shauinina asks if he's alright, and he replies, "I made love to the love of my life, of course I'm alright, get your beautiful self in this shower so we can start round two."

Chapter

9

At 7:00 PM sharp, everyone is in the dining room getting ready for dinner, but there is tension in the air, and everyone can feel it.

By 8:30, dinner is over, and all the dishes have been put away to be cleaned. Mom and Dad also put up any sharp objects just in case things go wrong. Dashan asks everyone to please go into the living room. He has something to say that concerns everyone. As everyone heads to the living room, Boné stops Dashan and asks him if he is sure about this decision, and Dashan says, "No, but it has to be done. I am tired of hiding who I am and what I have done." As everyone is seated and ready for Dashan to start talking, Sarai and Shauinina are discussing how her first time went, when Dashan kindly interrupts their conversation, "Excuse me, sis, I have to interrupt to talk to my wife."

Shauinina turns to listen to Dashan as he lays out the horrible details of their wedding night, and within a flash, Shauinina slaps Dashan and picks up a chair and bashes Latrain over the head with it repeatedly until Rah grabs her. Rah tells Shauinina to calm down before he has to make her calm down. Shauinina agrees, and then she proceeds to bash Dashan upside the head with the chair. That is when Rah loses it and starts choking Shauinina; TeeJay jumps in and breaks it up. Shauinina is so devastated that the only words that can come out of her mouth are "I want a DIVORCE."

She tells Latrain that she is going to kill her real soon, because she is nothing but a man stealing slut. Everyone is on edge and shocked because his family that just came have no clue as to why Shauinina is so overly upset with Dashan, but TeeJay fills everyone in on the past events and now there is understanding, Dad grabs Dashan and is about to throw him into the wall again when his brother Silver stops him and tells him there is nothing he can do it, has to be Dashan who has to fix this mess and besides he can't be injuring "the one" before 12 PM. Dad agrees to what Silver is saying and gives Dashan a pass for now but promises him that by 1:00 AM they will be fighting.

Dashan begs for his wife's forgiveness and for his family's also, but no one is trying to hear that right now they are more concerned about Shauinina and Latrain. Boné notices that Latrain is slumped over and not breathing well and notices that there is a lot more blood than before.

LeLe screams, "Shauinina no, what have you done?!"

As everybody looked, they noticed that Rah had his gun pointed at Shauinina, telling her, "Please don't make me kill you."

Dashan looks at his brother. "Put your gun down, Rah, or we will have major problems."

"We already have major problems," responded Rah.

Then, Boné tells LeLe to call 911, and she does. Now, Dashan has to figure out a way to get the knife out of Shauinina's hand before the cops come and not become victim number two. TeeJay walks up to Shauinina and tells her to put the knife down before she gets hurt really badly and goes to jail for a long time.

Shauinina just laughs. "What could be worse than what I am already going through. I told her from the last time we fought to leave my man alone, or else she would die. The only regret I have is that I couldn't get you, Dashan, my dear, but believe me, your time is coming soon."

Shauinina drops the knife and walks out the front door just as the police and ambulance arrives, nobody tries to stop her because they know how to deal with Shauinina once she regains her senses. The police have questions about how Latrain got stabbed 12 times and everyone said that she was found on the porch, once Latrain was out of surgery and conscience the police asked her the same question and she gave the same answer as everyone else, she said that she was drunk and don't remember nothing except being on the porch. Silver tells TeeJay to try and find Shauinina before 12 PM.

Chapter

10

BACK STORY

Shauinina Jackquie, who has an Associate Degree in Business, lives with her three cousins, Sarai, who is a bank manager, LeLe, who has an Associate Degree in Finance, and Latrain, who has an Associate Degree in Literature. She lives in Detroit, Michigan. They are very close, but the cousins are about to part ways to start their new lives. LeLe wants Shauinina to leave and move with them, but she can't because she still has a great job that she doesn't want to lose, and plus, she's not ready to pick up and start over just yet. The day is going to be kinda sad because she has to go to work instead of seeing her cousins off at the airport.

As Shauinina heads into the corporate building, she smiles at the doorman, Mr. James. He's been working for the corporation since he was 21 years old. Mr. James knows what today is and kindly tells Shauinina that she shouldn't worry about her cousins, they will be alright, and to cheer up because today is the day that everyone gets their yearly bonuses. Shauinina just laughs and tells Mr. James, "Now I feel better."

As soon as she is seated at her desk, her boss informs her that they will be having a meeting with a new client from out of town, marking the beginning of a major contract worth millions of dollars. Shauinina knows this meeting will be very long and boring, as most of them are, so she starts preparing the paperwork for the new client when there is a knock on her boss's door.

Shauinina leaves her desk to see who it is, but all she can see is the back of a tall Black man. When she gets close enough to him to ask if he needs any help, her boss opens the door and lets the mysterious man in.

As Shauinina returns to her desk, she catches only a glimpse of him and notices he has the most beautiful blue eyes she has ever seen, even if they are contacts. Her boss calls her into the office so she can give the client the paperwork to sign. As she enters, Dashan puts on his sunglasses because of the strong smell of lavender; his head is starting to hurt, and he doesn't want to be rude by just leaving. Shauinina introduces herself to Dashan, and he gladly shakes her hand, backing away to sit in the chair in the far corner of the office. Shauinina's boss asks if he's alright, and Dashan quietly responds, "I have a headache, and the bright sun isn't helping any." The boss quickly tells Shauinina to close the blinds and to get the client some aspirin for his head. Dashan tells Shauinina that it's alright and that just closing the blinds will be fine, so she does just that. Shauinina and her boss go over the contract with Dashan and ask if there is anything he would like to add or remove. Dashan tells them that everything looks fine, that he's very happy with the contract terms, and asks if he can have a glass of water. The boss tells Shauinina to go get it, but Dashan asks the boss if she can get him some water instead. Dashan just wants to savor Shauinina's scent, but it is so strong that he must ask her if she is wearing any perfume, to which she responds, "No, just soap and water." Shauinina then tells him that his contacts are very pretty.

Dashan starts to laugh and says, "Those are not contacts; they are my real eyes." Shauinina apologizes for the comment and quickly leaves the office just as her boss comes in.

The rest of the day goes by slowly for Shauinina, and she can't wait to get home to check if her cousins made it safely and to tell them about the new client with the beautiful blue eyes. Shauinina's boss asks her to call the client and ask him to come back to the office because he forgot to sign one of the documents. She does so, but then asks her boss for his information to call him, and all her boss provides is a business card with his last name on it. Shauinina calls Dashan and informs him that he needs to come back to the office to sign the last document, and he agrees to return only if she will be there. Shauinina agrees to stay late until he arrives. Shauinina checks the clock; it's after 5:30, and still no Dashan, so she tries to call him to ask how much longer he will be, but he doesn't answer, even though he looked at his phone and saw who was calling him.

Dashan is very curious about Shauinina for two reasons: first, she has a strange scent that he hasn't encountered before; second, he can't read her mind. Around 6:00, Dashan arrives at the office, and the only people there are Shauinina, Dashan, and Mr. James. Dashan apologizes for making her stay late, signs the papers, and walks out with her and Mr. James. Shauinina wishes everyone goodnight and safe travels home. Dashan simply smiles and tells her to do the same, aware that this will be the last time they see each other since he bought the building and plans to tear it down in two months. He feels guilty for not informing Shauinina or her boss about his intentions for the building, as the contract was meant to finalize the sale without her boss knowing. Little do they both realize that the events unfolding will ultimately lead them to one another.

By the time they find Shauinina, who is at the park, it is 11:30 PM, and Rah asks her to please come to the house so that Dashan can talk to her.

She looks at Rah and says, "Why should I be the one to go to him? Why doesn't he come to me?"

Rah calls Dashan and tells him that Shauinina wants him to come to her instead, Dashan agrees to her terms, but as soon as he is about to walk out the door his parents and grandparents stop him and tell him that their meeting will have to wait because time is getting short and they have more important things to tend to. Dashan asks, "What is more important than making up with his wife?" Dashan heads towards the door, but his uncle Silver stops him and tells him to please wait until tomorrow to talk with Shauinina, there are more important things to handle now, and that after 12 PM, he will understand everything. Dashan calls Rah back and tell him, "Please let my wife know that I will make everything up to her tomorrow, right now we have very important family matters to tend to."

Rah tells Shauinina what Dashan said, and she just laughed and walked away, saying," Exactly as always, I come second, never mind. I will go home, . . . oops, I mean over to my cousin's house for the night, and maybe tomorrow will be a better day."

Chapter

11

At 12:00 AM, a black Lincoln Navigator pulls up to the house, and four Black people get out and go inside. Everyone knows who they are except for Dashan. Mommy and Dad introduce the Elders to Dashan as they look him over one by one.

Dashan walks over and tries to see their faces, but they laugh and say, "Dashan, my son, the time will soon come when we will reveal ourselves to you, but for now, you are the 'one' who will rule over the whole vampire clan."

Dashan politely declines, "That's why we have ya'll to watch over all of us."

One of the Elders says, "He has the power, but hasn't used it yet."

Dad tells Dashan that he has to prove himself to the Elders, and Dashan replies, "So be it."

The first test is the blood thirst. One of the Elders leaves and returns with someone covered in a sheet, and when the Elder takes off the sheet, they see it's Sarai tied up and bleeding. Boné loses his mind because no one told him about using his wife as a blood sacrifice.

"What the hell is going on? Why is my wife here

and bleeding?!" Uncle Silver moves over to Boné and tells him to be quiet, but Boné refuses to listen and starts to walk towards Sarai when all of a sudden, he's gently pushed into a wall and held there, but no one is touching him. He now understands and just hopes Sarai isn't used as a sacrifice. The Elder laughs and says, "Your wife will be alright, if not, we will make you a new wife" (laughs).

Dashan doesn't like this but knows not to challenge the Elders, not just yet. The Elder takes Sarai's blood and rubs it under Dashan's nose and on his lips to see if he will try to taste it and feed on Sarai. Dashan knows that he can't feed from Sarai because he will lose all his humanity and morals. So, what he does is bite the inside of his cheek so that his blood is already on his tongue to make sure that he doesn't taste Sarai's blood. He then proceeds to lick the blood from his lips and walks over to Sarai and tells her to please forgive him. She looks up at him, confused and scared, as he winks at her. Dashan leans in and bites her on the shoulder and starts to suck up her blood.

Boné screams "NOOOO!!!" as he watches his wife fall over dead.

Dashan walks over to him and tells him, "I love you, please forgive me." Boné just hangs his head and cries. Dashan lifts his head, and he notices that his eyes are still blue, but his fangs are stained red with blood - he's confused.

Dashan whispers to him, "Use your mind, not your heart, and set yourself free."

You see, the one thing the Elders can't control is a hybrid's mind because of the human side. Dashan closes his eyes, and when he opens them, they have changed to a bright red and Gold. The Elders are happy with the outcome and proceed with the next test. The Elders tell Rah to put Sarai outside to be disposed of. With his head hung low, he cries as he carries her body to be buried; he gently lays her by the trash. Rah returns, and the Elder tells him to put his gun on the kitchen table and sit down. Rah hesitates, but the Elder raises his hand, and Rah has no choice but to obey. The second test arrives when an Elder walks over to Dashan's momma and tells her to stand in the middle of the living room; she does. Then, the Elder tells Silver to strip her naked and have sex with her.

Momma laughs, "The hell he will!"

Dad moves in front of his wife, but is instantly thrown in the kitchen. But just then, one Elder apologizes and tells Dad, "You will watch."

The entire family is furious and does everything to prevent this from happening, but no one can move.

Silver starts to beg the Elders, "Please don't make me do this, I'll do anything, please not this."

"The only one who can stop this is Dashan," one Elder says.

Dashan's eyes turn pitch black, and he roars with his fangs out and claws extended, "Use your mind and not your heart." All of a sudden, everyone can move again except for the purebloods, but the boys can.

They race to save their momma and lock her away in the basement for safety. The Elders are very surprised and very proud of Dashan. They know the vampire race is in good hands. The Elders released everyone else and told Dashan that he had passed the test. One of the Elders also told Dashan's Dad to get his wife out of the basement, she's in no harm. Dashan is still upset, but changes his feelings when everyone kneels down to him; he now knows he's the vampire ruler.

Rah tells Boné that Sarai is alive and well; they had to make the Elders think she was dead. Boné is relieved that his wife is okay, but he knows she is not really alright.

Boné asks, "Can I see her?"

Dashan tells him that it is not possible right now, and Uncle Silver urges Dashan to tell Boné the truth, explaining that it will hurt, but he will understand.

Dashan turns away from his brother with tears in his eyes, saying, "I can't do that."

TeeJay tells Boné, "The truth is that you cannot contact Sarai because Uncle Silver and I had to erase her memory, so she has no knowledge of anyone—not even her cousins. It's not permanent; it will only last for a year."

Boné breaks down and cries while the whole family comforts him; they know they have a lot of work to do. One of the tasks is to tell Sarai's cousins that she has left town due to the stress of Boné cheating and the impending divorce. Dad tells Boné that he has to keep seeing Lisa to avoid raising suspicion, because the Elders will be trying to use their powers to read everyone's mind to see if there is any information they can use to change their minds about Dashan being the "one." Boné reluctantly agrees and proceeds to call Lisa to arrange a date night.

As the family tries to get back to being somewhat normal, Dashan knows that he and Shauinina have to talk; he kinda wishes that it was her instead of Sarai, then things would be so much easier, but so much for wishful thinking. Just as he is about to call Shauinina, Rah tells him that all of them should be together when the news about Sarai is told. Dashan agrees, hoping that it will lighten the worries of their relationship and marriage.

Bone calls the girls over, and as they walk into the house, Mom notices that they all have a worried look on their faces. She asks them, "What's wrong, babies?"

Shauinina speaks and says, "Sarai hasn't been home in two days, and she's not answering her phone, Boné." She continues, "I know ya'll aren't vibing right now, but if you know anything, can you please tell us, or at least tell her to call us so we don't have to worry about her."

The whole family turns and looks at Boné, and he responds, "I wish I could, but she hasn't called me either." He then quickly leaves the room and goes upstairs to his bedroom to cry. He hates that this is happening, and lying to them hurts even more. Seeing that no one wants to really tell them what happened, Uncle Silver steps up and tells them.

"Ladies, Sarai is alright. She has left town because it is too much for her to deal with, her losing the only man that she has ever loved to another woman, and the fact that her marriage will be over with the signing of divorce papers." Uncle Silver continues, "Sarai will be in touch with ya'll soon. She just needs some alone time to find herself and to figure out if she and Boné can save their marriage with the test of time."

LeLe and Latrain cry, but they are very understanding and agree to let her live her life and hopefully come back home to her family. Shauinina, on the other hand, is not having it; she yells, "Bone, get down here! I know you had more to do with this than what Uncle Silver is saying."

Boné came downstairs with a look of hatred in his

eyes as he leers over Shauinina, "What do you want, woman? I am not responsible for your grown-ass cousin leaving me, or ya'll. She made her choice, now live with it . . . I have to."

Chapter

12

Boné walks back upstairs, but not before Shauinina jumps on his back and starts to beat him on the head while screaming at the top of her lungs, "It's all your fault, you just had to cheat!!!"

TeeJay grabs Shauinina and tells her to calm down. She does as she's told but still stares at Boné with hatred. Dashan yells, "Enough Shauinina, sit down and shut up before I put your butt out!"

Shauinina just laughs and responds, "Try it and I'll own everything, including you. See, I'm not like Sarai. I'm not going to run away, I'll make your life a living hell before that happens, and let's not forget I still owe you and your little side piece more pain."

Latrain begins to move closer to TeeJay and Rah. They notice and let her know that she is safe with them. Dashan has had enough and makes a rash decision to punish Shauinina by putting her in the torture chamber. He grabs her and carries her to the basement, leads her through a secret door, and tells her that this is the beginning of her learning how to act like a lady and behave like a woman, and the wife of royalty. Shauinina just laughs until she sees all the weapons and chains and torture equipment, then she realizes that he's lost his mind. She tries to run, but he's too fast and catches her and locks her up in chains, and ties her mouth shut with a red and gold rag. Dashan tells her she will learn to listen or pay the consequences with her blood and obedience.

Shauinina is starting to get very scared because she now knows that something is not right with her husband, he has never been this mad and mean to her before. She has to think of a way to make Dashan trust her so she can escape and get to some weapons to fight him, but she knows good'n well that if she fights Dashan and his brothers are around, then she will not be able to win or get her revenge. So, she sets her plan in motion to get Dashan alone to fight him, and hopes she will not be killed by him or his family once they find out that she has no reason to trust any of them ever again.

She knows they are all responsible for her cousin leaving without a trace.

Dashan comes down to check on Shauinina and to make sure she understands that she has to watch her mouth and calm down with all of the cussing, and trying to kill everyone who she thinks is responsible for her pain and heartbreak. Shauinina sees Dashan and calmly waits for him to remove the mouth gag so she can talk to him and try to persuade him to let her go.

Dashan looks at her and smiles, "Are you ready to behave, love?" He slowly removes the gag from her mouth so she can respond.

"Yes, my love, I am ready to behave, and I am sorry for trying to beat you up."

As Dashan removes her restraints, she looks around the basement to see if she can find something to knock Dashan out with so she can get something stronger to fight with. Just as she is about to grab a vase to hit Dashan, Rah comes downstairs and smiles at her, saying, "You are a little firecracker with murder intentions (lol)."

Shauinina doesn't answer him, but keeps her eyes on the vase. Rah moves in front of her and starts to laugh, "Please don't even try it. I like you, and it would make me very sad to have to kill you."

Shauinina just lowers her head and looks defeated, but as soon as Dashan moves in front of her, she tries to kick him in the private, and before she can even blink, Dashan has his hands wrapped around her throat, squeezing until she passes out.

"We need to tell Shauinina something so she can get this revenge out of her mind, because I don't want to kill your beautiful wife, or you end up choking her to death," says Rah.

Dashan agrees with him and comes up with a plan to have her and Sarai meet so she can feel somewhat better. Dashan brings Shauinina upstairs from the dungeon, lays her on the couch and tells the family his plan to have the cousins meet. Uncle Silver interferes and says, "How is that going to work when I have already erased her memory for a year? If we bring them together too, soon it will do more harm than good. I know you want your wife to feel whole again, but we are going to have to work a little bit harder to make Shauinina understand that Sarai just needs a little more time to heal, and if she continues to try to attack us she herself will not be able to heal from all of her hurt and pain that she and you have not worked out."

Dashan agrees with his uncle, and Shauinina awakens instantly, rushing towards her husband and trying to fight him, screaming and crying. Dashan just holds her real tight and lets her have this moment. When she finally calms down, he begins to speak slowly. "My love, please understand that you have the right to be upset and all the other feelings you are experiencing at this moment, but know that we are all hurting, not just you."

Shauinina looks around the room and sees that everyone is sad and hurting, but the pain that she sees in Bonés eyes makes her heart melt. She walks over to him and tells him how sorry she is, and to please forgive her for acting like a crazy woman. She would never want to hurt any of them, and to know that she will not be acting out of character unless it is to fight for and with her family, not against them.

"Will all of you please forgive me for being blinded with revenge and hurt?" Everyone hugs her and tells her that all is forgiven.

Shauinina turns to her husband and tells him, "Look, we have things to work out, and I am willing to work them out with you. I don't want to lose my husband, and we have the best family in the world."

Dashan just smiles and agrees with her, and with that, all is somewhat normal and less hectic, well, he hopes for now.

Chapter

13

Everyone has had a long day, and now it's time to eat dinner and try to relax, but it is kinda hard when there is so much going on. And one thing that the family doesn't like to do is lie to those who mean so much to them.

Latrain asks if she can talk to Dashan for a moment; everyone turns to look at Shauinina, and she nods her head, saying it's alright. Latrain and Dashan go into the backyard so that no one can hear what they are talking about.

Dashan asks, "What is so important that you want to talk to me about?"

Latrain starts to cry but keeps it together somewhat, "I am in love with you, Dashan. I know that it is wrong and that my life is hanging on by a thread, and right now, I really don't care. I know that you love me also, . . . It's just that you can't be with me because you're married and you want your marriage to work."

Dashan stops Latrain by getting in her face and slightly choking her. "If you ever try to do anything to wreck my marriage, I will personally kill you. I don't forget or forgive as easily, just remember that Latrain."

Dashan squeezes a little more, and Latrain passes out on the lawn in the backyard, and Dashan just leaves her there, returning to the house to continue dinner. Everyone notices that only Dashan has returned, and Mom asks, "Is everything alright son? You look very upset."

Dashan responds with a sly smirk on his face, "Yes, Momma, everything is fine and will be as soon as I take out the trash, because it's starting to get on my nerves."

Latrain returns and says goodnight to everyone and leaves to go home.

Dashan's phone is buzzing. He looks down at the message from Latrain:

"You may win tonight, but believe me this is not over, I will have you for myself. And if I have to make your life with Shauinina a living hell, then so be it! You want to war? Well, this is the beginning of war! Let's see if you can sweet-talk your way out of this one like you have done before . . . And oh, by the way, I have something in place for your wife - if she ever touches me again, she will be the one who will die, . . . Your move, love."

Dashan excuses himself and lets everyone know that he needs to go for a jog; he feels sleepy from all of the good food he just ate. Afterwards, he changes clothes and leaves the house, heading for Latrain's place. Once he gets there, she answers the door with nothing on and all smiles. Dashan just grabs her and smiles back as he proceeds to hug her and whisper sweet nothings in her ear. She notices that he is squeezing her a little too tightly, and that it's hard for her to breathe. She tries to get him to let her go, but he just keeps on holding her tighter and tighter.

Right before she passes out, Dashan tells her, "This is the end of you, and now who has won the war? You must have forgotten that I love to fight and win every time. Please believe me that you won't last this round."

As she passes out, Dashan just carries her out of the house and into the basement of his, where he has her tied up in this torture chamber, ready to have fun with his prey before he has to kill her for good, and then spin some kind of story as to why she is dead.

Dashan is having fun torturing Latrain and seeing the blood and pain he is causing her, but something inside of him is telling him to stop before he goes too far and there is no turning back, Latrain tries to fight and pleads with him to let her go, but there is no pleading with Dashan. She knows that soon she will die in the hands of her lover.

Dashan gives her a kiss and says, "What we had was good and fun, but you wanted to ruin my life, and now you see that you've ruined yours."

Just as soon as Dashan is about to end her life with a blow to the head, he hears his uncle inside his, telling him, "Don't do this nephew, because you are not going to be able to come back from this. Don't you feel it? It's not you, and you're not going to give in to this darkness. Yes, killing her will end some of your problems, but you are going to create more hurt and more problems for all of us."

Dashan decides not to kill her and releases her, but then he has another idea. Instead of releasing her, he will let her hang down there for a couple of days so she can understand that she is playing with the master, not a fledgling.

He then mentally answers his uncle, "I

understand. I will not kill her now, I'll just let her stew for a while."

When Dashan returns to the house, he sees everyone is looking at Boné funny.

"What's wrong now?" LeLe speaks.

"Boné is steadily declining with everything in his body. He doesn't want to eat, and all he does is work and doesn't sleep well. Please help him, we fear that he is going to die."

Dashan just sighs and looks at Bone, and asks him, "Is that what you want to do, huh? You want to give up and die, for what? A little time apart from your wife is what you want and need, right?"

Boné turns around and punches Dashan so hard in the face that two of his teeth fall out, and Dashan just laughs and asks, "Is that the best you can do, brother?"

Boné responds, "Naw, I have more for your crazy ass!" And proceeds to knock all the rest of his front teeth out, and with a quick reflex of speed, breaks Dashan's nose and one of his arms. Rah breaks it up and laughs because he knows that Boné can easily hurt Dashan, but he notices that Dashan is not even mad; he just keeps laughing like nothing is bothering him, and the fact that he wants more.

TeeJay notices it also and sends the girls home so that they don't get hurt. TeeJay is also making sure they are safe there, as well.

When LeLe asks where Latrain is, he responds by saying, "Oh, she texted me saying that she's bored and needs some fun, so she will be home in a couple of days."

TeeJay returns back to his home to find Dashan still laughing, and Boné still trying to kill his brother. TeeJay asks, "What the hell is going on with you, Dashan? You never would've said that to Boné, but now it seems like you have lost any compassion you have."

Dashan looks at TeeJay and says, "If he wants to die, then let him die with some sense and not just because he doesn't have his wife with him at this moment."

Rah notices that the air has shifted when Dashan and Boné are fighting. He quickly scanned the inside of the house, and when he went to scan the outside of the house, he noticed a black SUV in front of the house. Rah instantly knew who it was. He quickly went back inside and made the signal for everyone to be quiet, and then he went into Dashan's bedroom and quickly texted:

"The Elders are watching."

Everyone got the message, then Boné and Dashan understood what was happening and causing them to fight. They immediately started laughing and playing, using their mind and not their hearts. The front door opens, and the whole family walks out on the porch and begins to sit down, staring at the black SUV, letting them know that they are aware of the Elders' presence.

The SUV started up and pulled away from the house. Rah calls the girls just to check on them and to ask if everyone is alright; they answer, "Yes, just worried about ya'll."

Rah puts the phone on speaker, and the whole family responds, "We are all good, love ya'll, goodnight."

TeeJay asks Dashan how his mouth feels with teeth missing, and Dashan tells him, "I'm alright. I am going to the dentist in the morning to get some new teeth surgically implanted before I really start to feel the pain, and then beat Boné to a pulp," then laughs.

Everyone goes to bed feeling better and relieved.

Chapter

14

There's one thing that no one knows about: by morning, Dashan will have new teeth. He also has the ability to block people out of his mind at any given time.

Just as Dashan is about to lay his head down, he remembers that Latrain is in the dungeon. He's too tired to go get her out, so he leaves her until morning.

It's 4 PM the next day, and Uncle Silver goes down to the basement, opens the door to the dungeon, and finds Latrain barely alive. He takes her down and sneaks her out the back to his rental car so he can take her to the doctor. While at the hospital, Boné sees his uncle and tells him that one day, Latrain is going to end up dead between Dashan and Shauinina. Uncle Silver just nervously laughs and agrees. Boné says she's free to go home, and Uncle Silver asks, "Should I wipe her memory?"

Boné nods no. "Just let her use this as a possible lesson to leave Dashan alone, hopefully."

On the ride home, Uncle Silver tells Latrain, "You need to let the idea of you and my nephew ever being a couple go. It's not going to end well for you, and I don't want that to happen. Think of other people besides yourself."

Latrain looks out the window and says, "I will never give up on love or Dashan, even if it costs me my life. Believe me, if I can't have him, neither will she. Both of our lives will be full of pain and misery if I don't get my way."

Uncle Silver drops her off and tells her, "Be safe. No matter what you decide, just know it will be more than just you and Shauinina getting hurt if anything ever happens to my nephew, Latrain." Then Uncle Silver walks into the house and sees Dashan. "Nephew, I took the trash out for you when I cleaned the basement."

Dashan nods in understanding.

Uncle Silver let Dashan know about the conversation with Latrain in the car, and Dashan lets him know it is not going to be easy to get rid of her so soon, but her time will be coming and it's a shame because he really did like Latrain and was hoping that they could put the past behind and become a real family. But, oh well, this is her life and her decisions to end it.

Dashan gathers the family together, the girls included, because he has some important news to let everyone know about.

"Family, I have called you all together because I have made a decision to embark on a new adventure in my and my wife's life. We are moving into our own home."

Everyone looks at him like he's speaking a foreign language. Shauinina is happy because she wants nothing more than to have a peaceful and happy life with her husband, minus his family.

Rah speaks, "Did Shauinina threaten you?"

Everyone just laughs. Mom and Dad agree that it's time for everyone to find their own way in this world.

"We have also been thinking about moving, and we want to go back home to Nigeria to live out the rest of our lives."

Everyone is not alright with the decisions that are being made so suddenly.

Boné speaks out abruptly, "What about my wife, Sarai? Where am I supposed to go in case she comes home? I know her time is almost up, and I want her to come home to a familiar place."

TeeJay lets Boné know, "Don't worry brother, you

and Sarai are all taken care of. You just need to pick out a house or a piece of land, and your house will be available for you and her."

The girls ask, "We are going to miss ya'll, but do what makes you happy and just know that if anyone needs us, we will always be here."

TeeJay looks at LeLe. "You are not staying in that apartment either, you and Rah will have ya'll own place just like everyone else. Please don't think that we would ever leave you beautiful ladies behind. You are family."

Boné tells everyone that they have a lot of work to do and to make sure by the end of the month, they have places and lots planned out. Dashan tells everyone that within two months, everything should be in place for everyone.

He then walks over to Latrain and whispers, "Make sure you put where you want to be buried."

Latrain loses it and starts to cry and yelling, "I don't care if you kill me, Dashan, just know that I won't go down without a fight! And best believe your life will be pure hell until I get what I want, which is you!"

Shauinina just laughs. "Poor Latrain . . . Girl, let it

go. I ain't going to waste no more of my time and energy fighting you, and my husband ain't either."

Latrain just turns around and begins to leave. Then she paused for just a second, tilting her head in angle, while shrugging her shoulders and cutting her eye as if she didn't give a damn. "Believe me, cousin, you will regret marrying him. And Dashan, you will be full of hurt and pain when I am through with you unless you give me what I desire."

Then Latrain continued to walk off until Rah quickly snatched her shoulder back. "I am sick of you! I should break your neck right now, but I won't because you have people that love you, but if you ever threaten my brother, I will make good on my promise, or . . . (with a sinister expression on his face, looking her up and down) should I get rid of the trash now?"

Latrain shuts up, not even trying to give any backtalk to receive more than just another beatdown, because she knows just how dangerous Rah is, and that if she even tries to move to speak, he will kill her. Yeah, it's about that time for everyone to go their separate ways and plan their new life for better days.

Chapter

15

Meanwhile, about a mile away in Haggard Parks, there is a very unique young lady named Saym. She is a witch hybrid, but she doesn't know anything about her parents, only what she has read in the newspaper. Saym is having a hard time sleeping because she keeps hearing someone calling her for help. She gets up and goes outside onto the porch to get some fresh air, and she can hear the voice more clearly, as if it's right behind her.

She closes her eyes and asks, "Who or what are you?" There is nothing outside but silence and the sound of the nightlife. As she goes back inside her apartment, she notices a figure in her recliner chair. She approaches it, but the figure fades, though the voice continues asking for her help. Saym goes into her bedroom and returns with a black book. She relaxes and tries to make the figure more solid so she can at least understand what species it is, and how to properly deal with it, whether it's bad or good.

The figure is composed of embers and smoke, so she grabs a blanket to throw over it in an attempt to put it out, but the figure disappears again. She searches through the black book for anything that could help the figure, coming across a spell to help materialize it. The next time the figure appears, she performs the spell. And to her shock, it materializes into a person that only those in her circle whisper about, someone she never believed was real. There is a big burst of smoke and fire as CHAOS materializes into his old self.

"Hello, Saym. No, you're not dreaming. It is really me, and I need you to help me get to the Elders. I have some very important information they need to know about. After that, you and I can have a nice dinner and get more acquainted with each other. I promise to answer any questions that you may have. But first, my dear, do you have a car?"

Saym is so shocked that she forgets how to speak. When she finally does, the only thing she can come up with is "CHAOS."

He laughs and replies, "Yes, it's really me in the flesh, so to speak. Now, dear, do you have a car or a phone?"

Saym gives him her cell phone for his call, but he doesn't use it. "What's wrong? Let me guess, you don't know how to use a cell phone?"

Chaos answers, "No, I need you to make the call for me, dear, by using your powers, please?" Saym agrees to contact the Elders for Chaos.

Once the call is made, they wait for the Elders to arrive. Upon their arrival, one of the Elders stared directly at Chaos, and under his breath in a very low distinct, high-pitched animalistic nature growled in anger, as if he was howling, when they arrived. Chaos tells Saym to stay in the house and wait for him. He then gets into the black SUV and tells them everything that has happened to him and the Wilson family, including what they did to him, and how he can get in touch with his crew to finish off the brothers.

The Elders tell Chaos that they are aware of the fight and the whole incident at the warehouse. "We told you to kidnap Dashan and bring him to us, not to try to kill his brother. You almost cost everyone their lives because of your desire to be the vampire king. You just don't listen, and you never will unless you are made to listen. We could've brought you back when the time was right, but no, you want to do things your way and involve the witch Saym, who we had under very watchful eyes.

Now she has opened the black book and here you are."

The Elder with the white eyes spoke, "You don't have to worry about the vampire clan being in jeopardy, we have a new king, and his name is Dashan Wilson."

Chaos was mad and very disappointed because that was supposed to be his title. He calmed down and started to speak very slowly and carefully.

"I understand your reasons for doing what you thought was the right thing to do, but I have some information for you that will change everything you thought you knew about the Wilson family."

The Elder with the white eyes look Chaos in the eyes while crushing his windpipe. "There is nothing that you can tell us that we don't already know, Chaos. We know you are full of hate and will do anything to become the vampire king, but that will never happen. And if you don't watch your tone, this time you won't even be able to come back as nothing, you'll be just a name that is whispered, as always. If you don't believe me, try me . . . Please, I beg of you, Chaos."

To be continued . . .

RIGHT BEFORE CHAOS VANISHES INTO THE AIR, HE TURNS AND TELLS THE ELDERS THAT . . .

"BY THE WAY, THE HUMAN THAT WAS SUPPOSED TO BE DISPOSED OF, IS ALIVE. YOU MIGHT WANT TO CHECK INTO THAT SITUATION."

CHAOS THEN VANISHES INTO ASHES.